My Big Book
of
Grimm's Fairy Tales

PUBLISHED BY: PETER HADDOCK LTD,
BRIDLINGTON, ENGLAND
ILLUSTRATIONS BY: JORDI BUSQUET
STORIES ADAPTED BY: ISABEL URUENA
GRAPHIC DESIGN BY: JUAN FRANCISCO RAMOS
INTEREDICIONES, J. M. ©
TYPESETTING BY: PRINT-OUT (HULL) LTD.,
PRINTED IN: USSR

The Crystal
Coffin

A clever little tailor set out to see the world and one night came to a leafy forest where he soon became lost.

"When daylight comes I'll be able to see my way out of here, but for now I'm going to find a place to sleep," he said.

He climbed up a tree and from there he spied a light and thought it could be a house. He clambered down the tree and set off towards it.

It was a little, wooden cottage and inside he could see a candle burning.

The little tailor knocked on the door and it was opened by a little, old man.

"Who are you and what do you want?" he asked.

"I am a tailor and I've lost my way in the forest," answered the young man.

"Please, I beg of you to let me spend the night in your cottage."

"Go away, I don't want any tramps in here!" shouted the old man as he pushed the door shut. But our tailor begged so hard that the old man, who was not really hard-hearted, let him in.

After they had both eaten, the tailor settled himself on a wooden bench and fell asleep at once. He was very tired.

Next morning he was woken by a strange noise. He ran outside the cottage to see what was happening; a large bull was fighting with an equally large stag. Their hoof blows made the earth shake. The stag finally killed the bull and left it where it fell. Then the stag lunged at our friend and catching him on its antlers rushed off through the countryside.

The tailor clutched on to the stag's antlers with all his might in order not to fall off; they were going so fast it seemed as though they were flying.

After a few hours they came to a wall and there the stag set the bewildered tailor down upon the ground.

"Such strange things are happening to me!" he said to himself.

The stag then began to butt its antlers against a door in the wall until it opened and a ghastly column of smoke began to appear from within.

The young tailor did not know whether to remain or to flee but just then he heard a voice from the vault which said:

"Come in! Come in! You will not be harmed!"

As he was a plucky boy he entered the vault and the smoke quickly disappeared.

There was a large room with a great stone in the centre. It was covered in strange signs and writing which the tailor could not understand no matter how hard he tried. The voice spoke again:

"Be seated on the stone and fortune will smile upon you."

He sat upon the stone and it began to sink to the floor below just like a hoist. By this means he came to another room, much larger than the one before. In its centre there stood a transparent crystal coffin. The tailor looked down at it and

saw that inside a beautiful young maiden was sleeping; she was dressed in rich riding clothes crowned by a mass of blonde tresses. The tailor was dreamily watching her, when suddenly the maiden opened her eyes and upon seeing him exclaimed:

"Please, open the lock on the coffin and the wicked spell will be broken."

The little tailor did just that and the young maiden pushed open the lid of the crystal coffin and climbed out. She then walked over to a corner of the room where she found a large velvet cape which she put on. Then she made her way to the stone which was now low enough for her and sat upon it.

"Come, sit beside me and I'll tell you my story," said she.

"My parents died some time ago. My brother and I were very close and never thought of being parted until one day a foreigner asked to spend the night in our castle. We begged him to stay for a few days as he seemed very nice. One evening he told me that he wanted me for his wife. Then he began to demonstrate his evil powers. He cast magic spells and changed roses into lizards, cats into statues and other things that I can't remember," said she.

"I had no desire to marry, especially a wizard. But when I told him so he flew into a rage and ran off," said the princess.

"The following day I looked all over the palace for my brother but I could not find him anywhere. I asked the foreigner if he had seen him and by way of an answer he laughed in my face and told me that I would never see my brother again if I did not marry him," she said.

"Then, I don't know why, I dressed in my riding clothes and went to search the woods for my beloved brother.

There, I met the horrible wizard who was leading a handsome stag by a rope. He told me that the animal was my brother.

I took out my pistol and fired at him but the bullet bounced off his chest and killed my horse. Whereupon, I fell to the ground and was knocked unconscious," said she.

"When I awoke I found myself locked inside this crystal coffin and the wizard was standing next to it. Again he told me that the stag was my brother and that the palace and all my servants had been turned into smoke and locked inside the crystal bottles.

Everything would be returned to normal if I agreed to marry him, but I still refused. He told me that only a suitor chosen by my brother could break the spell. As my poor brother was now a stag I did not expect him to be able to

find a suitor. Then I slept. I dreamed that a young man came to my rescue. As soon as I saw you I realised you were he," sighed the maiden. "Finally all our misfortunes appeared to be coming to an end," she added.

"Now, let's set all my servants free." So the princess began to uncork all the bottles.

Coloured smoke began to pour from them and it quickly turned into the princess's maids and butlers.

Once they were all free only one bottle remained unopened: it was a large bottle which contained the castle itself. They all climbed on to a large stone to uncork it. The palace began to grow before their eyes until it reached its proper size.

Then each servant, happy to be back to normal, went again to work in the palace. The stag, which had earlier been locked in combat with the bull and had carried the tailor on its antlers to the vault, suddenly appeared before the little princess and her rescuer.

The maiden kissed it on the forehead and the animal once again became her beloved brother whom she hugged lovingly.

"The bull which you saw me fighting to the death was the evil wizard who caused us so much harm.

At last he's dead and you have saved us. Nothing more remains for me to do but to thank you and ask you to take the hand of my sister, the little princess, in marriage."

The tailor naturally accepted the prince's proposal with

great joy as the young maiden was worthy of any sacrifice and, enjoying the gifts God had bestowed upon them, they all lived happily ever after.

The Four Clever Brothers

There was once a man who had four sons. When they were grown up he said to them:

"My sons, it is now time you went out into the world. As we are poor I can give you nothing. Learn a trade, you are all clever enough, and I'm sure you will make something of your lives."

The four brothers hugged their father and set out on the road.

Presently they came to a place where four roads crossed and each took a different path.

"It's time for us to part," said the eldest brother.

"Let each one of us go our own separate way and within four years all return here and tell of our adventures. Until then, let each one follow his own path."

After walking alone for a while the first brother met a wayfarer.

"Hello my boy!" said the man. "Where are you going?"

"I'm going to learn a trade," answered the youth.

"Then come with me and I'll teach you to be a thief."

"No, that's not an honourable trade and you always end up in jail," answered the youth.

"Don't be afraid. I'll teach you how to steal the way no-one else can."

The man finally convinced him and the young man learned to be a clever thief taking whatever he wanted without any danger to himself.

The second brother met another man and after talking to him for a while admitted that he did not really know what trade to follow.

"Then come with me and I'll teach you to be an astronomer," said the man. "It's a delightful trade and with my telescopes you can see incredible things that no-one else can see." The youth was satisfied and went with the man and learned all that he could

learn about astronomy. When he became a good astronomer his master presented him with a fantastic spy-glass and said:

"With this spy-glass you can see everything there is to see in the heavens and on earth, no matter how far away they are."

The third brother met a hunter and as he was a clever lad he profited greatly from his lessons and in the end he bade farewell to his master, who presented him with a sturdy bow and said:

"With it you will always hit the target of your choice. You'll never miss."

The youngest of the brothers stumbled into a wayfarer and after talking to him for a while told him that he wished to learn a trade.

"What about being a tailor like me?" asked the man.

"Well no. I think spending every day seated at a table, sewing, would be very boring. I'm not eager to do that," answered the boy.

"What nonsense! I'll teach you to be very different from any tailor that you've ever known and you'll be famous. Be assured, you won't be bored!"

In the end the youth accepted the offer and for a while studied the tailor's trade. He was hard-working and on leaving, his master said to him:

"Take this needle; with it you can sew anything whether it's as hard as steel or as delicate as a spider's thread. And the stitches you sew will never be seen."

Four years had already gone by and the four brothers met at the place where the four paths crossed and from where each one had made his own way in life. They greeted each other joyfully and together they walked to their old father's house where he awaited them happily.

"All together again! I want you to tell me what you have been doing these past four years."

One by one the young men told of their adventures of which we already know. When they had finished speaking their father walked with them to the door of the house and said:

"You, my son, have learned to gaze at the heavens and the earth. Can you see those eggs in that bird's nest at the top of the pine tree?"

The astronomer took his spy-glass, looked at the tree and said: "There are five eggs in the nest."

"Well done," said his father. "And you, you say you are able cunningly to steal whatever you want; see if you can steal those five eggs from the little bird which is sitting on them without it knowing what you're about."

The thief climbed the tree and came down with the five eggs in his hand. The little bird had not even noticed him and continued to sit there. Then their father placed the five eggs on the garden table; one at each corner and the fifth in the middle.

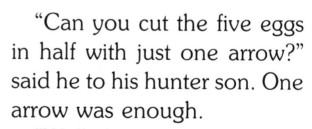

"Can you cut the five eggs in half with just one arrow?" said he to his hunter son. One arrow was enough.

"Well done. Now you, my son, can you sew the eggs together without leaving any trace?" said his father.

The little tailor took out his needle and sewed up the eggs delicately and swiftly. The thief returned them to the nest and within a few days little chicks hatched out and the mother bird, who knew nothing of what had happened, sat happily to the end.

The old man was proud of his sons and rightly so. He was certain that with their ability the four brothers would become famous one day.

Shortly afterwards a terrible disaster struck that land; the princess was carried off by a fearsome dragon. The king became desperate as no-one dared to rescue her. Finally he published a proclamation in which he promised the maiden's hand in marriage to anyone who would save her.

"Boys, this is just the opportunity for you!" said their father.

The astronomer took out his spy-glass, looked about him and finally said:

"I can see her, I can see her! She's on a rock in the middle of the sea and the dragon is next to her and it's watching her."

The four brothers asked the king for a boat and sailed off in search of the princess. It did not take them long to reach the rock. The dragon

was sleeping with its head cradled in the princess's lap.

"I can't shoot it," said the hunter, "for if I do I will also kill the maiden."

"Fear not. I'm going to try to get her," said the thief.

He swam to the rock and with very great care spirited the princess from under the dragon's head. Together they swam to the boat where the others greeted them joyfully. But just at that moment the dragon awoke and saw the princess sailing away in the boat. Now the dragon had a pair of wings and it flew towards the boat roaring and blowing fire from its mouth. The hunter brother took aim and his arrow pierced its heart. But as the enormous body fell into the water it caused the boat to break in two and sink into the depths of the sea.

The brothers and the princess were marooned in the middle of the ocean clinging to some planks. They were all beginning to weep when the tailor brother took out his magic needle and began to stitch together the wreckage floating in the water. Within a few moments he had rebuilt the boat and no-one even noticed the stitches.

Now they were able to
return to their own land.
When the king saw them sail
into view with his daughter
safe and sound he leaped into
the air with joy. After hugging
his daughter, he said:

"One of you must wed my daughter. Decide who is to be the lucky one!"

The brothers began to discuss it among themselves.

"I saw her first! Without me you would never have found her. I will marry her," said the astronomer.

"I got her away from the rock without the dragon noticing it! Who else could have done that? I will be her husband," said the thief.

But the hunter did not agree:

"I slew the dragon! Without me it would have eaten us all. I am going to marry the princess, you owe your lives to me."

The tailor said:

"I stitched the boat together! If I had not remade it we would all have drowned. I will be the princess's husband."

The king saw that the four brothers could not agree and therefore he made this suggestion:

"I can see that you four are my daughter's rescuers, as you have all played an important part in this adventure. But as she cannot marry all four of you it would be better not to marry any one of you. I will give each of you a part of my kingdom as a reward."

The brothers accepted the king's reward and ceased their squabbling.

"Besides, who knows if we would have been happy marrying the princess. We hardly know her . . ." they thought to themselves.

The king rewarded each one of them with a castle surrounded by lands and they all lived happily with their father for many years.

The Three Spinners

Once upon a time there was a very idle girl who never wanted to spin. Her mother used to scold and punish her and try to reason with her, but it was all in vain, she did not want to spin.

One day her mother completely lost her patience and slapped the girl who began to scream loudly. Just at that moment the kind-hearted queen was passing by in her royal coach and upon hearing the child's cries drew up to the house to see what was happening.

"Why are you hitting the child so?" said the queen. The girl's mother did not know where to put herself.

"I am ashamed to tell you that I have to smack my daughter because she will not do as she is told," answered her mother, not wishing to tell why she had scolded her.

"I know how difficult children can be at times, so please tell me," answered the queen.

The mother did not want to admit that her daughter was idle so she said to the queen:

"I can't let her go on spinning. She spends all day spinning as she doesn't know how to do anything else. Besides, I'm a poor woman, I don't have the money to buy all the yarn she needs. That girl's going to ruin me . . ."

"What a happy coincidence!" exclaimed the queen, clapping her hands. "There is nothing in the world I like better to hear than the sound of spinning. Let me take your daughter to the palace, and there she can spin to her heart's content.

I have enough money to buy more yarn than she could spin in a lifetime."

In spite of the child's pleas the woman let the queen take her daughter to the palace. Upon arriving, the queen led the girl to a room which was completely full of yarn and said to her:

"Now begin spinning and when you have spun all this yarn you may marry my son. It doesn't matter if you are penniless, for you are a hard-working girl and have no need of money."

The girl was very shaken for she knew she could not spin that yarn in three hundred centuries. When she was alone she began to cry bitter tears. She cried for three full days. On the third day, the queen entered to see how her work was progressing.

"What! Haven't you done anything yet?" asked the queen with surprise.

"Well, actually I'm missing my mother," said the girl.

"Yes, I can see that. Never mind, get down to work, you can't still be so homesick," said the queen as she left.

The girl did not know what to do. She did not like spinning and besides it was useless to try; that mountain of yarn could not be spun easily.

As she was feeling lonely she looked out of the window and saw three women walking towards the palace.

The first woman had a very big right foot. The second had such a large bottom lip that it hung down in an ugly fashion. The third's thumb on her right hand was like an enormous spoon.

The women looked up at the window and called to the girl who was watching them:

"What's wrong, little girl? Your eyes are very red, have you been crying?"

"The queen has told me to spin a room full of yarn and I don't know how to do it. If only I could do it I would become the prince's bride. But it's useless to talk of it for all this yarn could not be spun in centuries," answered the girl.

"We will spin the yarn if you will invite us to your wedding. We know that we are ugly, but you must not be ashamed of us and must call us your dear cousins," said one of them to her.

41

"I promise!" exclaimed the girl. "Come, begin now."

The three women entered the room and began work. The first turned the wheel with her foot; that is why it was so big. The second wet the yarn with her lip; that is why it was so heavy. The third twisted the yarn with her fat thumb; that is why it looked like a wooden spoon.

When the queen came to see how the work was going the girl hid the three spinners behind a mountain of yarn and showed her the fine skeins that were already spun. The queen said:

"What a hard-working girl! I've never seen anything like it! My son will be your husband, you are truly worthy of him."

In just one week all the yarn in that immense room had been spun.

Not even the girl who had seen it all spun could really believe it. In truth it was hardly possible to imagine the speed with which those three women worked.

Once they had finished the three women prepared to leave and said, "Don't forget what you promised us. We will return on your wedding day so that you can present your husband to us as if we were your cousins. We only want to tell you that if you do what you promised, you will find happiness."

The girl showed the queen the empty room and all the skeins piled up against the wall and the queen, who was a woman of her word, said: "Tomorrow we will begin to prepare for the wedding."

The prince was delighted to be betrothed to such a hard-working girl as she was also very pretty and clever.

When it was time to send out the invitations the girl's thoughts went back to the spinners and she said to her bridegroom:

"I have three cousins and I love them dearly, they are very special to me. You just cannot imagine how much they have done for me. I would love them to come to my wedding and sit at my table. After my mother, they are the family I love most of all."

"Say no more!" answered the prince. "If you wish them to sit at our table, there they shall sit. We will reserve three places."

The day of the wedding arrived.

It was the wedding of the crown prince and representatives of every land came to pay their respects; each one dressed more richly than the one before. The girl and her bridegroom looked radiant.

After the wedding ceremony all the guests stood back to let the three spinners pass. The women were smartly but modestly dressed. They reached the bride and groom's table and were respectfully greeted by the girl.

"These are the cousins I've told you so much about," she said to the queen and to her new husband.

"Come, sit with us!"

How ugly they are! thought the prince to himself.

Then, the young bride-groom asked the eldest of his wife's cousins:

"Why is your foot so big?"

"With so much spinning, so

much spinning . . ." she answered.

Then he leaned over to her second cousin and said:

"And you, why do you have such a large, hanging lip?"

"With so much spinning, so much spinning . . .!" she answered.

Finally he asked her third cousin:

"Your thumb, why is it like that?"

"Well, with so much spinning!" answered the woman. "My eldest sister turns the spinning wheel with her foot. The second one wets the thread with her lip and I spin it with my thumb."

The prince spent his meal in thought and when the banquet was over and everyone had gone home he said to his mother, the queen, in front of his bride:

"I don't want my beloved wife ever to touch a spinning wheel again!"

This is the story of how a girl was spared from spinning for the rest of her life. As you well know, a king's orders must always be obeyed.

The
Three Little Dwarves
of the Wood

In the same village there lived a widow and a widower. They both had a daughter. The two daughters were friends and played together. One evening, the widow said to the little girl who was the widower's daughter:

"Tell your father that if he married me I would treat you very well, better than my own daughter: you could wash yourself in milk while my daughter would only wash in water."

So the girl told her father and he agreed to marry the widow.

In the beginning everything went smoothly and the woman looked after both girls equally well. But after a short while he noticed that she did not love her stepdaughter at all. While the man's daughter was very beautiful and well-mannered the woman's daughter was quite ugly and unpleasant.

One snowy winter's day the woman made a paper dress and gave it to her stepdaughter saying:

"Put on this dress, go out into the woods and bring me a basket of strawberries."

"Goodness me, but it's so cold!" cried the girl.

"How can I go out in such a thin, little dress? Besides, strawberries don't grow in winter so I won't be able to find any . . ."

"Do not answer me back, do as you are told!" screamed the woman.

She gave the girl a tiny piece of bread to eat and led her to the door. She hoped that the girl would become lost in the woods.

As the girl walked through the woods she saw a tiny house between snow-covered trees and three little dwarves looking at her through the window. She knocked at the door and the dwarves invited her to warm herself by the fire. Then the girl took out her piece of bread.

"Will you give us a bit?" said the dwarves.

"Yes of course I will!" answered the girl as she shared out the bread.

"What are you doing in the woods wearing such a flimsy dress?"

"I have to collect strawberries and I can't go back home until I've filled this basket," answered the girl.

The dwarves asked the girl to sweep clean the back door. There, under the snow, she found a mountain of strawberries. After filling her basket she said goodbye to the dwarves and made her way back home. The dwarves began to talk about her and said:

"What shall we give her for sharing her bread with us?"

"I will make her more beautiful every day," said one.

"Every time that she speaks I will make gold coins fall from her mouth," said the second.

"I will make a king fall in love with her and take her away to his palace," said the third.

The girl arrived home and as she said "Hello" gold coins fell from her mouth.

"How wasteful!" cried her stepsister. "I want to go out into the woods to look for strawberries."

Dressed in a fur coat and with a basket full of cakes, she left to find the dwarves' house.

The girl found the house and saw the dwarves looking out of the window.

Instead of knocking on the door, she walked in without being invited, and sat down near the fire. She took out the cakes and began to eat them.

"Will you give us a little cake?" said the dwarves.

"No! I only have a few and I want them all for myself," she answered.

When she had finished eating the dwarves said to her:

"Take this broom and sweep behind the house."

"Sweep? Certainly not!" said the girl arrogantly, slamming the door behind her. The dwarves began to talk among themselves saying:

"What shall we do with this rude and selfish girl?"

"I will make her more ugly every day," said one.

"Every time that she speaks, toads and snakes will slide from her mouth," said the other.

"I will see to it that she dies," said the third.

The girl looked round the house for strawberries but found none so she returned home. Once there she wanted to tell them what had happened but as she did so, toads and snakes began to slide out of her mouth and everyone moved away from her in horror.

The wicked stepmother was angry with her husband's daughter, but she did not know what to do to pay her back and make her life a misery.

One day she said to the girl:

"Take this bucket to the river and rinse the sheets in the water."

As the girl knelt down by the river bank a carriage came by and inside it was the king, who was a handsome youth. Upon seeing the girl he ordered his carriage to stop.

"Who are you and what are you doing here?"

"I am a poor orphan and I'm rinsing this linen," she answered. The king was captivated by her beauty and said to her:

"Would you like to come with me to my palace?"

"Oh yes!" answered the girl who was happy to leave the cruel stepmother who had made her suffer so.

Upon arriving at the palace they became betrothed and on the following day they were married.

A year later the young queen gave birth to a child. When her stepmother heard of her good fortune she was so mad with envy that she decided to do something about it. One day while the king was away she went to the palace with her daughter. They crept to the queen's chamber and caught her by surprise. After tying her hand and foot they threw her out of the window into the stream which ran by the castle. The stepmother put her own daughter into the bed, drew the curtains and told everyone that the queen was very ill and no-one could see her.

When the king returned she said to him:

"Be quiet! You can't talk to the queen now, she has a raging fever!"

"God be with her!" said the king anxiously. "Look after her well and you will be rewarded. I'll return tomorrow."

But that same night, a wild duck entered the palace kitchen and said to the young servant:

"What is my little boy doing?"
The servant answered:
"He's fast asleep."
Then the duck turned into the young queen and went up to feed her son.

Then she tucked him up well and before dawn, went back down to the stream and once again was changed into a duck.

This happened on a number of nights. A week had passed and the queen learned that the king was very sad. He believed she was ill and wished with all his heart to see her.

"Tell the king to go down to the gate with his sword, and wave

it over my head three times," said the queen to her faithful servant.

When the king received the message he ran down with sword in hand. At the palace gate he awaited the wild duck and then waved his sword over its head three times. After the third time the duck again changed into the happy and healthy queen.

The king was overjoyed to have his beloved wife back safe and sound.

As for the two intruders, the queen was powerless to stop the king from giving them just what they deserved he ordered them both to be thrown from the window into the stream and they were never heard of again.

The young king and queen lived a happy and undisturbed life ever after with their little son and their lives were always peaceful.

Fearless John

Once upon a time there was a man who had two sons. The elder was very bright, whereas the younger was thought of as a fool because he had little interest in anything. His name was John. Well no, not exactly, there was something that he wanted to learn, but no-one was able to teach him. He wanted to learn how to tremble with fright. The lad spent every day nattering to his father, "Yes, what you tell me is easy enough to understand, but what is fear? I want to learn how to tremble with fright."

"To tremble?" his father exclaimed angrily.

"Go away, I don't want to see you again. Take these coins and may God protect you."

So John went off, always looking for someone who could teach him how to tremble with fright. One night as he was dining at an inn, he said to the innkeeper:

"Listen, my good man; I don't know what it is to tremble with fright. I would like someone to teach me. Do you know anyone who could do it?"

"I know the very place!" exclaimed the innkeeper. "Nearby there is an enchanted castle, full of treasures which are guarded by devilish spirits. If you are able to spend three nights there, you will discover what fear is. The king has promised his daughter's hand in marriage to anyone who can endure three nights there. You see, the princess is in the castle under a spell. Many knights have tried but not one has returned alive."

"Don't tell the child such things," said the innkeeper's wife.

"It would be terrible if those lovely, bright eyes never saw the light of day again! Don't go, lad, you're much too young."

But John had decided. The next day, he went to the king and said:

"Your Majesty, I want to spend three nights in the enchanted castle and rescue your daughter and your treasures."

The king thought John an honest lad and answered him thus:

"It is done. If you are successful, you shall have my daughter for your wife. If you wish you may take three objects with you to the castle."

"Well, I would like wood for the fire, a potter's wheel and a carpenter's bench with a knife," said John.

As night fell the young man made his way toward the castle; the three objects that he had requested were already there. He went into one of the rooms and lit a cheerful fire. He put the carpenter's bench in front of the bonfire and sat down at the potter's wheel.

"How happy I would be if only I could learn to tremble!" said he to himself.

All of a sudden he began to hear moaning and barking. From the four corners of the room rabid dogs and cats leaped onto the fire and tried to frighten John with their antics. John remained seated and was very calm. At last he tired of the racket and, picking up his knife, he struck right and left and frightened them all away.

It was already late and he was so tired that he slumped onto a bed in the corner. As soon as he had settled down to sleep the bed began to move; to run from one side to another as if it was alive. It somersaulted and buried John under a pile of blankets and pillows. John slid out from under the bed, made himself a bed of pillows on the floor near to the fire and slept peacefully until the next day.

The king entered the castle. He felt sorry for that pleasant lad whom he did not expect to see again, when suddenly he heard John say to him:

"Hey! I'm over here! I did sleep well!"

"Haven't you learned to tremble yet?" asked the monarch.
"Well, no . . . Perhaps I'll have more luck tonight."
On the second night John heard a loud clanking of chains. After
a while, half of a man's body fell down the chimney in front of him.

71

"Hello! This is a bit mean, isn't it?" said the boy.

The other half of the body fell noisily down. The two halves joined together to form the revolting figure of a man-monster, but John was not at all worried. He was not even worried when through the door came some men as ugly as the first, and began to play skittles with bones and skulls.

"Can I play too?" asked John.

"Yes, if you have any money," they answered.

"I have money, but all your bowls are not completely round. I'll make them round so they'll roll better."

He picked up the skulls and smoothed them with the carpenter's plane so that they were round and smooth. Then he played until twelve, which was the hour when the men and the bones disappeared. John then went back to bed.

And that is how the king found him next morning.

"How did you spend last night?" he asked him.

"I played skittles and I lost some money, but I still don't know what it's like to tremble," said the young man.

The third and last night, while John was stoking the fire, four men entered the room carrying a coffin on their shoulders. John walked up to the body in the coffin and seated himself by the fire with the corpse cradled in his arms.

"I'll warm you up, just you see," he said to the corpse.

He rubbed its arms and legs. But as the dead man did not get any warmer, he placed him in bed and climbed in beside him. After a short while the dead man began to warm up and then to move.

"You see you are not so cold any longer, are you?" said John.

"Hold fast, I'm going to strangle you!" cursed the dead man leaping up in a flash.

"Is that how you thank me? Well, you can get back in your box!"

As he said those words he pushed him until he fell back into the coffin. The four men carried him back the way they had come.

"As you can see I'm still not trembling," said John to himself.

Suddenly a horrible-looking old man with a large beard appeared.

"I'm going to kill you," he said to John. "Tremble! Take this hatchet and prepare to fight me."

The old man, split an iron anvil in two, such was his strength.

"Can you do that?" he asked.

"Yes, but come closer so you can see me better," answered John.

When the old man was next to the anvil, John swung the hatchet and trapped the old man's beard in the split in the anvil. The old man stamped and kicked but he could not escape. John gave him a good thrashing until he begged for mercy.

"I'll tell you where the castle's treasures are! I'll tell you which vault the princess is locked up in!" repeated the old man.

John set him free and the old man led him to the castle vaults. There were many chests full of gold and from behind a wall, which the old man demolished with one blow, appeared the captive princess. The old man disappeared with the dawn while the princess and John awaited the king, who was swiftly at their side.

"You have broken the castle's spell and you will marry my daughter!" said the happy monarch.

Within a few short days the couple were married. John

loved his wife dearly, but from time to time she heard him say:

"Oh, if only I knew what it was to tremble . . .!"

Until one day his wife, who also loved him dearly, got fed up with his complaining.

"He always says the same thing, and I don't know how I can help him! What can I do?" said she to her chief chambermaid, who was a very clever woman.

"I'll show you how you can teach him to tremble," answered the chief chambermaid.

One night, on the instructions of her faithful servant, the young queen crept down to the garden with a jar in her hand. She scooped up water and little fishes from the pond and returned to her chambers. There she lifted the covers off John, who was sleeping soundly, and poured over him the water and the little fishes, which leaped all over John's back, tickling him until he woke up shouting:

"I'm trembling, dear wife! What a shock you've given me! At last I know what it is like to tremble!"

The Fisherman and His Wife

M any, many years ago on a lonely North Sea headland stood a worthless hut. In that hut lived a fisherman and his wife. Every day the man would sit on a rock and cast his line. The few fish that he caught were sold in the village market, and that is how he got by.

One day after fishing only a short while, he felt a sharp tug which bent his rod in two. The float bobbed once, then twice and the fisherman pulled with all his might. An enormous fish appeared and tried to free itself from his hook by thrashing wildly about in the water. The man was greatly surprised when he heard the fish say:

"Please, let me go! Spare my life. I am not an ordinary fish, as you can see. I am

really an enchanted prince under an evil witch's spell. If you let me go, you won't regret it."

"All right, I am no good at dealing with fishes that talk, so you can go if you want," answered the fisherman throwing the fish back

The grateful fish plunged down into the depths of the sea. That evening, the fisherman told his wife what had happened.

"And didn't you think to ask it for anything in

exchange for its freedom?" she asked.

"Well, to tell the truth, I didn't," answered the man. "And besides, what could I ask it for?"

"Don't you know?" said his wife. "Here we are living in poverty, anything it could give us would be welcome. Go back and if you see it again tell it I want a cottage. If it really is a prince then that is not too much to ask . . ."

The fisherman returned to the rock and waited there a while.

But it began to grow dark and, as the fish had not taken the bait as before, he started to sob loudly. The fish was not far away and when it heard him it poked its head out of the water.

"What do you want of me?" asked the fish.

"Forgive me for bothering you, but my wife wants me to ask you for a favour," said the fisherman.

"It is easy for me to grant what you desire. But the next time you need me, sing this little ditty:

Fishy, fish, fish,

Please, come near,

My wife, Alice, has a wish,

Which you must hear."

"Yes, I'll do that. But all we want you to do is to turn our worthless hut into a nice cottage."

"It is done. Go home and see," replied the enchanted prince. By the time the man got home his hut had been completely transformed. His wife was waiting for him at the door. However, their contentment did not last long because the following day, the fisherman's wife began to complain.

"This cottage isn't as comfortable as it seemed. The rooms and the garden are too small. I would prefer to live in a mighty stone castle with plenty of room. You'll have to go and see the prince again and ask him for it."

The fisherman did not really believe it was the right thing to do but, as the fish had been so friendly, he went to the rock and began to sing the ditty.

"Fishy, fish, fish,
Please, come near,
My wife, Alice, has a wish,
Which you must hear."
As quick as a flash the fish appeared before the man.
"Here I am, what do you desire?"

"I don't want to bother you, but my wife has been nattering so. She would like a mighty stone castle instead of a cottage," answered the fisherman.

"You're not bothering me. Go back home, your wife's wish is fulfilled," said the fish.

The man returned home to an enormous castle. At its gate, standing in regal gardens, was his wife. They toured the castle together and

saw that it had been furnished with exquisite taste. Every room had its own servant awaiting their command.

At the rear of the castle there was a dense wood full of animals, and a stable full of beautiful horses. How they feasted their eyes upon such riches!

Alas, after a few days, the fisherman's wife began to search the castle for her husband in order to have words with him.

"I want you to go back to the sea shore and call for the enchanted prince. I want to be queen," said Alice.

"That is impossible! Anyway, why do you want to be queen? Haven't you already got everything you want?"

"It's good to see you're a man and you'll put up with anything!" said the woman sharply.

The fisherman saw that a tremendous row was brewing, so he did as he wife had told him and went to the sea shore and began to sing the ditty:

"Fishy, fish, fish
Please, come near,
My wife, Alice, has a wish,
Which you must hear."

Upon singing those magic words the fish appeared from beneath the waves.

"Here I am. What do you desire?"

"I think this is going to be an impossible request," said the man hesitatingly.

"For me there is no such thing as impossible," answered the fish.
"Well, this time, my wife wants you to make her queen . . ."
"Don't worry. Go home, I've already granted your request,"
replied the creature.

On his way back the fisherman came across a troop of soldiers playing drums and trumpets. At the castle everyone talked of Her Gracious Majesty Alice. He went to look for her and found her seated upon a golden throne in the centre of a great hall. A large number of courtiers were bowing before her and the fisherman, to his own surprise, did likewise.

Time passed but the woman's ambition knew no bounds and after a few weeks she sent a minister to look for her husband as she wanted to talk to him urgently.

"I've got another request for your friend, the fish," she said to her husband.

"Another favour? Aren't you rich and powerful enough? Aren't you our queen? What more do you want?"

"It is true I am powerful, but I am annoyed because in the morning and in the evening the sun and moon come out without my permission. So, I want to be queen of the sun and the moon too."

The fisherman went to the rock more worried than ever before, and called for the prince:
"Fishy, fish, fish,
Please, come near,
My wife, Alice, has a wish,
Which you must hear."

The fish appeared but this time he was scowling at the fisherman.

"What do you want now?"

The man began to shake. He was just about to leave, but, fearing his wife's bad temper, he finally blurted out:

"My wife wishes to be queen of the sun and the moon," he said weakly.

"So, is that what she wants? Well, she can't!" shouted the fish furiously.

"Go home, it's not a palace any longer but the old hut you used to live in and be thankful that I haven't punished you for your greediness."

The fisherman said not a word. On his journey home his rich clothes gave way to the rags that he always wore. The gardens, the wood and the castle had all disappeared. In their place stood his miserable hut. Inside, he found his wife crying silently in the corner. She also had lost her lavish clothes. She was, once more, the wife of a poor fisherman.

"From now on," said the fisherman forcefully, "your greedy fantasies have come to an end. We will be poor all our lives. And while we are about it, I am going to tell you something else: I don't want to hear another word of complaint ever again."

It is said that his wife learned her lesson and even accepted her lot cheerfully and that they lived out the rest of their lives in that poor hut by the sea shore.

Beautiful Carnation

In a far off land there lived a king and queen who had no children although they dearly wished for them. One day the queen was strolling through the fields when a frog came up to her and said:

"Cheer up, young queen, soon you are going to have a son! He will be a lucky boy because whatever he desires shall be his."

The queen hurried home to tell the king and sure enough, one day, they had the child they so much wanted.

In the palace there was a large garden where the queen spent every day playing with her son. In various parts of the garden there were caged, wild animals. It was like a zoo.

Now the palace cook was a very ambitious man. He knew that the child got everything he desired and he decided to kidnap him. One day, while the queen was dozing and her son was busy making sand castles, the cook stealthily carried the little prince away and hid him in a secret place.

Then he returned to the garden, covered the sleeping queen's clothes and hands in blood and went straight to the king to accuse her of the child's murder.

"I saw her give your son to the fiercest animal in the garden, your majesty," said the treacherous cook, "so that the animal would eat him."

The king saw the queen
standing all alone and with
blood-stained clothes and believed the cook's lies. He was
angry with his wife and ordered her to be locked up in the
castle's highest tower and not
given any food.

The poor, innocent queen cried for her son and for the cruel way she had been locked in the tower by her husband. But, as God did not want her to die of starvation, he sent two doves to her cell window with food every day.

The years passed by. Finally one day the cook gave up work at the palace and said to the child who was still a youth:

"I would like a beautiful palace for myself, with gardens and woods. I want you to live there with me."

The child repeated the words and the cook's wish came true.

After a while, the cook noticed the child was becoming bored, and, fearing he wanted to go back to his parents, said to him:

"As you have the power, why don't you wish for a little girl to be a friend to play with you and keep you company?"

The prince's wish came true and a little girl of his own age and as sweet and pretty as a picture appeared before his eyes.

The two played together and as they grew older they began to love one another.

But fear haunted the cook. He had enough gold to last a life time without the child ever making another wish for him. But, as the prince grew, the cook became ever more afraid that he would turn against him. So one day, he spoke to the little girl and said:

"Tonight, while the prince sleeps, go to his chamber and thrust this knife into his heart. Then bring it back to me so that I can see that you really have obeyed my command."

"But how could I do such a thing to my beloved prince?" cried the horrified little girl.

The following day the cook became very angry with the little girl because she had failed to commit that horrible deed.

"I'll let you off this once, but if you don't do it tonight, I'll kill you myself tomorrow."

The little girl had a stag killed and its heart brought to her. She then said to the prince:

"Get into bed and listen to what he'll have to say about you."

The girl gave the cook the stag's heart on a plate and he exclaimed:

"At last you have done it! Is this the prince's heart? You have obeyed my command and in return I give you your life!"

Just then the prince leaped out of the bed.

"Confounded rascal! So you wanted to kill me! What have I done

to you to make you want to murder me? Well, now I'm going to turn you into a black dog with an iron chain always about your neck and you shall eat nothing but red hot coals."

After the boy had said those words, the cook turned into a horrible, black dog which was tied to a thick chain and ate nothing but red hot coals.

From then on the prince often thought about his mother and one day decided to go to his father's castle to see if she was still alive.

"Do you want to come with me?" he said to the little girl.

"I would only be a nuisance to you," she answered.

"If that is why you are worrying, then don't," replied the prince. "I'll turn you into a flower and I'll wear you always on my jacket."

The girl was turned into a beautiful carnation and the young man put her in his buttonhole so that she would always be with him.

He set off on his journey and soon reached the castle where his father still lived. He did not want the king to recognise him so he offered his services as a great pheasant hunter.

The king gave him employment as a hunter and on the following day the young man went out into the woods to hunt alone.

Once he was far enough away from the castle not to be seen, he wished that a hundred pheasants would appear in a row before him. They did and he killed them one by one. Then he put them in a sack and took them to his father. The king was most satisfied and rewarded him with gold coins.

As everyone now knew him as the king's favourite pheasant hunter, he took the opportunity one night to creep up to the tower where his mother was held prisoner. The sentry let him pass on the promise of a pheasant for himself.

His mother was old and weak but not yet dead. The prince said to her:

"Dear mother: I know how much you have suffered and I have come to save you. But I can't now release you myself; it must be my father who takes you from here and recognises your innocence."

After lovingly embracing each other the prince left her to put his plan into action.

The following day he returned to the woods and when he was well out of sight he wished that a thousand pheasants would appear in a row before him. They did and he killed them one by one.

Then he threw them into a hand-cart and off to the palace he went.

The king was very pleased with the young hunter who brought him pheasants from a wood where none had ever been seen.

Such was his delight that he organised a great pheasant feast for his closest courtiers and he also invited the hunter to sit beside him.

The young man desperately wanted someone to mention the subject of his mother and sure enough, someone did.

"Your Majesty, whatever happened to your wife?" said one of his courtiers, without thinking.

"She let a wild beast devour my son and I punished her for it," answered the monarch.

"That isn't true, father!" exclaimed the young man. "I am your son and this dog you see here is the cause of it all. When I command him to return to human form you will surely recognise him."

In front of all the guests the dog once again turned into the aged cook who had wrongfully accused the queen.

"I order you to tell the truth!" demanded the prince.

The cook was forced to admit his crime and the sorrowful king ordered his wife to be brought before him so that he could apologise to her. The kind-hearted queen generously forgave her husband and they tearfully embraced.

They were all fascinated by the young prince's description of his life with the evil cook.

"Do you wish to meet the young lady who refused to murder me

even though she put her own life in danger?"

"Yes, I would like to meet her," said the king.

Then he took the carnation out of his buttonhole and once again changed it into his playmate.

They all warmly welcomed the little maiden who soon after married her prince.

She became like a daughter to the king and queen and the four lived happily ever after.

Although, like everyone else, the young princess had a name, from that day forward she was always called BEAUTIFUL CARNATION.

The Water of Life

There once was a king who became gravely ill. His three sons were very sad as they knew that even the most famous doctors gave him no hope of recovery.

The three brothers were huddled on a garden bench sobbing when a little, old man came up to them and asked what had happened.

"Our father, the king, has an incurable illness," they answered. "There is one thing that will cure him," answered the old man. "It is the Water of Life. If he drinks it he will be cured. But it is hard to find . . ."

"I will go and look for it!" exclaimed the eldest brother, and went to ask his father's permission to set out.

"It is a dangerous task," said the king. "But if you have made up your mind, go."

The prince set off and thought to himself: "If I find the Water of Life, the king will give me his kingdom." Presently a tiny gnome stepped out in front of him and said: "Where are you going in such haste?"

"Get out of my way or I will flatten you under my horse. It is no business of yours where I'm going!"

The gnome cursed the prince, but the prince took no notice and galloped away into a gorge. The rocks at each side became narrower and narrower until his horse could not move. The haughty youngster was trapped and could not even get off his horse.

After a while those in the castle gave up hope of ever seeing him again. The second brother asked for the king's permission to search for the Water of Life and after much persuasion, he agreed. So one fine morning he set out on his trusty steed.

"If I succeed in bringing back the Water of Life, I will inherit his crown," he thought.

After a long ride he came across a tiny gnome who asked where he was going. But the prince answered in the same manner as his elder brother and the gnome cursed him. The horseman rode into a gorge which rapidly became narrower until he, too, was trapped.

Time went by and the youngest brother decided to set out in search of the Water of Life and he told his father so.

"My son, your brothers haven't returned and I don't want you also to disappear. But if it is your wish I won't stop you," said the king.

The youngest of the three princes left the palace that morning.
Presently he met the tiny gnome.
"Where are you going in such haste?" he said.
"I am going to look for the Water of Life," answered the youngest.
"And do you know where to find it?"
"No, I don't," confessed the boy.

"You are a pleasant lad and I am going to show you the way," said the gnome. "It gushes from a fountain within an enchanted castle. Take this iron bar and these two small loaves. You must hammer on the gate with the iron bar, and once you are inside, you will meet two ferocious lions. Give each one a loaf and they will leave you in peace. Then quickly find the fountain and leave the castle before the stroke of twelve, because then the gates close and you will be trapped inside."

The prince thanked the gnome and continued on his way.

When he came to the castle he did just as he had been told. He hammered on the gate with the iron bar and it opened wide. The

two ferocious lions which sprang at him calmed down when he threw them the small loaves. In the first chamber he entered there were several bewitched boys. He removed their rings and also took one of their swords and a loaf which was lying on the floor.

In the second chamber he was met by a beautiful maiden.

"Thank goodness I won't have to stay here for ever," she said. "You've saved me. In exactly one year, if you wish, I will marry you and we will reign over this land. Now I will tell you where the fountain is, but it is already eleven o'clock and you must not waste time."

The prince then thanked her and promised to return after one year.

In the third chamber there was a bed, and the young man fell upon it to rest. But he was soon asleep and did not wake until a quarter to twelve. He hurried to the fountain which the princess had told him about, poured the water into a flask and ran towards the gate as fast as he could and luckily just passed through it as the clock struck twelve. As the gate noisily closed behind him it tore a corner off his cape. The youngster climbed onto his horse and set off for the palace carrying the Water of Life.

He had just set out when he met the little gnome, who told him the following:

"The sword that you picked up will defeat any army. The bread that you are carrying will multiply and pacify the hunger of the largest town. Use these two things for everyone's good."

"Dear little gnome, I don't want to return home without my brothers. Do you know where they are?" asked the prince.

"I have punished them, but for you I will free them. Watch them, they are not to be trusted."

The three brothers met and set out for home together.

The youngest told the others what had happened to him and they were mad with envy.

As they passed through kingdoms stricken by famine and war, the young prince used his sword and magic bread to vanquish the enemy and feed the starving people. So much good did he do that he became their hero.

One night, while the youth slept, his brothers stole the flask holding the Water of Life and replaced it with a flask of sea water.

"We will give the king the Water of Life and he will prefer us to our brother," they said to each other. "And as for marrying this princess within a year, we will have to see . . ."

Upon arriving at their father's palace, the three offered him their flasks. First he drank from the youngest prince's flask and it almost killed him; it was sea water. Next he tried the water from the other brothers' flasks and was cured immediately.

The king was furious with his youngest son and banished him from the kingdom while he treated the two wicked sons like saints.

As the months passed the palace began to receive many gifts for the youngest son. They were gifts of gratitude; chests filled with jewels from those kingdoms which he had helped. The messengers of those lands told such stories of his youngest son's kindness that the king began to have doubts.

"Oh! Goodness me! Have I misjudged my son?" said the monarch.

So much was it on the king's mind that he decided to send messengers to the four corners of the earth to search for his youngest son and ask him to return to his palace.

Meanwhile, the year had passed. The two wicked brothers were bent upon marrying the princess at all costs, and set off separately for the castle.

The enchanted princess's servants had built a road of pure gold which ran up to the palace gate. Then she said to them:

"The knight who rides along this road of gold will be my promised one and you must let him pass. But if anyone approaches the castle by any other route, don't let him pass."

The eldest brother came into view. He saw the road of gold, and, not wanting his horse to ruin it, turned away and sought another path to the castle. When he arrived at the gate, the soldiers drove him away.

The second brother soon appeared. Just as he was about to gallop onto the road he saw it was paved with gold and pulled his horse up sharply so as not to ride over such riches.

He was greatly surprised when the soldiers at the gate refused to let him enter.

Within a few hours the young prince appeared happily riding to meet his beloved. He was so lost in thoughts of the princess that he did not even notice the golden carpet which covered the road and galloped over it up to the castle gate. It was after all the quickest route. The soldiers opened the gates and the princess welcomed him as her husband.

They were married that very same day. Then the prince and princess were crowned as monarchs of those lands.

In the middle of the wedding feast, presents and messages began to arrive from the prince's father, who greatly regretted his mistake and wished to make up with his son. The young couple travelled to see him and told him the true story of the Water of Life and how his brothers had taken it from him. The king wished to punish them, but they had fled from his kingdom never to return.

The king was content. After all, he had found his youngest son. And they all lived happily together for many years.

The
Goose-Girl

There was once a widowed queen who had a very beautiful daughter. While the child was growing up she was promised to the prince of a neighbouring country. The day of the wedding arrived and the princess was about to set off for her future husband's palace.

"I'm too old to go with you, but take this handkerchief, there are three of my tear drops upon it. It will protect you on your journey," said the old queen to her daughter.

The princess set out upon Falada, a horse which was able to speak like a human being. She was accompanied by her chambermaid, a second horse and a cart which contained her bride's dowry. Mother and daughter kissed and said farewell.

After riding for a while the princess became thirsty.

"Get off your horse, take my golden goblet and bring me water from the spring," said the princess to her chambermaid.

"If you're thirsty, then get down and get your own water," answered the woman.

As the princess did not wish to argue, she dismounted to fill her goblet with water from the fountain. But the chambermaid did not want to give her the golden goblet so she had to drink straight from the fountain. The little handkerchief given to her by her mother began to sing:

"If your mother knew,
it would break her heart in two . . ."

They rode on for some hours and the princess again became thirsty. She asked her chambermaid for water, but received the same arrogant answer as before and had to dismount and drink water from a stream. The princess did not notice, but her handkerchief dropped into the water and was carried downstream by the current. But the chambermaid had seen it.

"You've lost the lucky charm that protects you!" she shouted.

"Now we'll see who's the mistress here!"

When the princess returned to the horses she found the chambermaid already mounted on Falada's back.

"Give me your clothes and put on mine," ordered the wicked woman. "From now on I'm going to be the princess and you'll be my chambermaid. And if you so much as breathe a word of it to any living soul, I'll kill you myself. I swear it."

The poor princess was stricken with fear and swore to remain silent. Then they continued their journey towards her bridegroom's kingdom.

When they arrived at the prince's palace, they were joyfully received. The chambermaid, disguised as the princess, went up to her royal chambers, and the real princess remained in the courtyard. The king saw her from his window.

"Who is that beautiful young girl?" he asked.

"She's a beggar-woman, I picked her up along the road. If you have a place for her among your servants, then give her work," said the impostor.

"She can help the lad who looks after the geese," said the king who was a kind-hearted soul.

The false bride, fearing that Falada would tell all, spoke to the king at the first opportunity and said:

"I beg of you to order the beheading of my horse, it was such a nuisance to me on the way here that I don't want to see it again."

Then the palace slaughterman beheaded Falada. But the young princess learned of it and went to see the slaughterman.

"I'll give you these gold coins if you'll do me the favour of placing this horse's head on the town gate, so that every day when I take out the geese I'll be able to see it."

The slaughterman did just that. In the morning, Conradkin, the little goose-herd, and the princess passed underneath the horse's head and the young girl said:

"Oh dear Falada,
your head is hanging from a gate!"

And the head answered her:
"Oh dear, you beloved princess,
now a lady much less!
If your mother knew,
it would break her heart in two . . ."
The two youngsters and their geese went off to the meadow.

Once there, the princess untied her hair and began to comb it. It shone like purest gold in the sun and Conradkin, who was a playful boy, wanted to touch it. When the girl saw what he was about to do she sang:

"Blow wind, blow,
and off will Conradkin's cap go!"

A sudden breeze carried the boy's cap into the air and he had to run quickly to retrieve it. When he caught up with the princess, she had put her hair back under her straw hat and Conradkin could not touch it.

The same thing happened the next day; as they passed underneath Falada's head the girl said to him:

"Oh dear Falada,

your head is hanging from a gate."

And the head answered:

"Oh dear, you beloved princess,

now a lady much less,

if your mother knew,

it would break her heart in two . . ."

The young girl again untied her hair and began to comb it. When Conradkin tried to touch it, she sang:

"Blow, wind blow,

and off will Conradkin's cap go!"

The boy was rather annoyed by her pranks. When he returned to the palace he ran to the king and said:

"I don't want to go to the meadows with the new goose-girl."

"For what reason?" asked the king.

Then Conradkin told him of the strange things that he had seen. The king was intrigued, and ordered the girl to be brought forth to explain her mysterious behaviour.

"I can't tell you anything. I've sworn not to," answered the girl. "I can't tell you or any other living soul what happened to me."

The king begged her to tell him, but as the goose-girl would not give in, he said to her:

"If you won't tell me what happened, then why don't you tell your sorrows to this old fireplace?" And he walked off to his chambers.

When the princess saw that she was alone, she went to the fireplace and began to cry bitterly.

"This won't break my vow, because you're not a human being. And I must talk to someone . . ." said the sobbing child. "Here I am, far from my mother, forgotten by everyone, in spite of being the true princess! The wicked chambermaid who wears my clothes and who is going to marry my bridegroom has managed to turn me into a plain goose-girl. And as I cannot speak for fear of death, I'll have to live the rest of my life like this. If my mother, the queen, knew, it would break her heart in two!"

The aged king, who had been listening at the other side of the fireplace, in the next chamber, heard all her cries and much more. Then he realised who the little goose-girl really was.

He ordered rich clothes to be brought for the girl, and when she was dressed, he called his princely son and told him what he knew.

The young prince was speechless before the beauty of the true princess and he was delighted that the deception had been discovered before the marriage, otherwise, without knowing, he would have married the chambermaid.

The treacherous woman was locked in the dungeon for the rest of her life for attempting to take the true princess's place.

143

The prince and princess were married the following day and had a very happy and joyful wedding and they reigned over their kingdom when the old and wise king passed away.

Rumpelstiltskin

A miller and his beautiful daughter lived in a windmill.
One day the king passed by on a hunting expedition and
stopped at the mill to take a drink of water. Out of politeness, he
asked the miller about his work and his family. The miller, who
loved his daughter above all else, spoke of her proudly saying:

"I can't begin to tell you how wonderful my daughter is. She is so good at everything and whatever she spins turns into pure gold."

The selfish young king was most surprised and thought to himself:

This sounds worth my while! I'll see if the old man is telling the truth and if she can turn whatever she spins into gold I will always be rich.

Aloud, he said, "Old man, if this is true, your daughter ought to live in a palace not in a windmill. Bring her to my castle tomorrow and I'll put her to the test."

After the king had gone the miller told his daughter what he had said and she burst into tears.

"But, Daddy, you know I can't do that! When the king finds out, he'll be very angry with us," she cried.

"It's too late, we must go to the palace tomorrow.

We're in God's hands now," replied the miller.

Next day the king welcomed them cheerfully. He ordered the girl to be locked in a luxurious chamber with a spinning wheel and a mountain of straw.

"Right, get to work and turn this straw into gold as soon as you can. If you don't, I'll order you to be locked in a dark dungeon," said the king.

As soon as the girl was alone she began to cry hopelessly. Suddenly, she heard a voice next to her say:

"Why are you crying, my lovely? Why are you worrying so?"

It was a little gnome with a big beard. He wore a red, pointed hat and a pair of richly carved, wooden clogs.

"My father told the king that whatever I spin turns into gold and the king expects me to turn this straw into gold," replied the girl.

"Don't worry! I can do it for you," said the little gnome, "but, what will you give me in exchange?"

"I'll give you this pearl necklace!" said the girl.

The gnome began to spin the straw and sure enough turned it into pure gold. Then he took the pearl necklace, did a little somersault and disappeared.

Next day, when the king saw the mountain of gold he was speechless. He invited the girl to a sumptuous meal and was charming to her. But that evening he led her to a large chamber, where she found another spinning wheel and an even larger mountain of straw than before, and said to her:

"I wish you to do the same with all this straw."

"But Majesty, I . . .!" stammered the girl.

"If you refuse, I'll lock you up!" shouted the king.

As soon as the child was alone she began to cry.

"Who will help me now? Oh, dear me, I don't want to spend the rest of my life in a dungeon!"

Once again the gnome appeared before her.

"Why are you crying so, my lovely?"

"The king has commanded me to turn all this straw into gold but I can't."

"Fear not, I will do it for you, but what will you give me in exchange?" asked the little man.

"I'll give you this precious ring," said the child.

The gnome began to spin and by midnight all the straw was turned to gold. He took the ring from the girl's hand, somersaulted and disappeared into thin air.

Next day the king was beside himself with joy. He held a ball in the girl's honour. But, as night fell, he led her to an even more luxurious chamber than before where there was a spinning wheel and a gigantic mountain of straw.

"This is the last favour I'll ask of you. Please, turn this straw into gold. If you refuse, I'll lock you up," he said.

When the child saw all that straw she began to cry bitter tears. Once again the gnome appeared before her.

"Why are you crying now, my lovely?"

"The king has commanded me to change this mountain of straw into gold, but I don't know how to do it!"

"Don't fret, I will do it for you, but what will you give me in exchange?" asked the gnome.

"I have nothing left to give you," exclaimed the girl tearfully.

"Well, I will help you, but you must promise me one thing."

"What must I promise you?"

"That when you become queen your first child will be mine," replied the gnome.

As the child was a miller's daughter she never expected to be a queen, so she was perfectly happy to agree.

"Yes, I promise you," she said to the little man.

The gnome spun the straw late into the night. By sunrise he had finished the task.

He somersaulted and disappeared, as before.

When the king saw the gold he felt happier than any mortal on earth and asked for the hand of the girl who had made him rich.

"Yes, I'll marry you, if you promise never to ask me to turn anything else into gold," she said.

The king agreed as he was now a rich man and was truly in love with the girl.

They were married and a year later the couple had a beautiful baby son. The queen was so happy that she completely forgot the promise she had made until, one day, the gnome appeared before her.

"Hello! I have come for your son. Remember, you promised to give him to me and I need a servant."

"Please, I beg you, don't take him away from me. I'll give you all my treasures, but don't take my son."

She cried and begged, until at last the gnome said:

"I'll come and see you every night for three nights. If during these visits you can guess my name, I won't take your child."

Before the first visit, the queen memorised all the names she could think of and recited them to the gnome, who kept saying:

"No, not that one! No, that's not my name! Ha! ha! ha!"

Before the second visit the queen read lots of books, dictionaries and ancient manuscripts. But all to no avail.

"No, that's not my name!" answered the gnome repeatedly.

The queen was desperate. Only one more chance remained and she did not know what to do to guess the gnome's name. She told her problem to a good and faithful page.

"Don't worry, Your Majesty. I will try to find out his name," said the page.

The young page mounted a sturdy steed and galloped out of the castle and did not return until the following morning. The he went straight to the queen and told her this story:

"I rode through the magic wood all night. When it struck midnight, I saw a little gnome standing by a fire. He was wearing a red hat and singing

this song:
    "Tomorrow, I'll be fine,
    the prince will be mine,
    and the queen will pine,
    and she will find,
    That Rumpelstiltskin is my name."

The queen was overjoyed when she heard this and generously rewarded her faithful page. Then she awaited the gnome's third visit.

"Your name is . . . Rudolf," said she.

"No, that's not my name! Ha! ha! ha!"

"Then is your name Conrad?" asked the queen cleverly.

"No! no! You're getting colder and colder!"

"Then it can only be Rumpelstiltskin!" cried the young mother suddenly.

The gnome was amazed. Then in an angry voice he shouted:

"A witch has told you, a witch has told you. Curse you . . .!"

He was in such a rage and kicked the ground so hard that he made a hole in it through which he tumbled.

From that day forth, the queen lived happily and peacefully with her husband and son and was never again bothered by the evil gnome.

The Six Swans

There was once a king who loved hunting. One day he became lost following a wild boar. He was very tired, so when he spied an old woman, he said to her:

"Old lady, I am lost in this wood and as I am very tired, I would like to know which is the shortest route out of here."

"I will tell you if you promise to fulfil one condition," said the old woman who was really a witch.

"What is the condition?" asked the king.

"You must marry my daughter. She is so beautiful she deserves to be queen."

As he had no alternative, the king agreed, and within a few days he married the witch's daughter. She was beautiful, but the king was rather frightened of her. So he called together the six boys and one girl that he had from a previous marriage and took them to a secret castle out of his new wife's way.

He visited the royal children so often that the queen became suspicious and decided to follow him.

She watched as the king was led to the castle by a magic ball of wool which unravelled itself and guided him. When the wool was completely unwound it stopped at the castle where the seven children were hidden.

The queen watched as the six boys came out to greet the king; then she returned to the castle without arousing the king's suspicion.

Within a few days, the wicked queen had woven six singlets with a special thread which her mother had given her. When they were finished she stole her husband's magic ball and was led to the secret castle. Once there, she found the six boys playing in the garden and forced the singlets upon them.

The boys were immediately turned into six swans. Then she returned home, convinced that she had settled her husband's children for good.

As the queen had not seen the king's daughter, the maiden had been spared her wicked spell. The little girl was watching out of a window when her beloved brothers turned into swans and flew up into the sky. She cried bitterly at the queen's wicked deed.

When the king returned to see his children the little princess told him what had happened, but she was afraid to tell him that the queen was responsible for their misery.

"Don't worry father. I will go and look for my brothers and rescue them," said his daughter.

She set out next morning. After walking all day she came to a little cottage and went inside to rest. There were six identical beds and she sank down onto one of them. Later she heard a loud noise; it was the beating of wings. Then six swans came into the cottage and changed to human form: her six brothers. They were overjoyed and they hugged her.

"You can't stay here, little sister! The people who live in this cottage are rogues. They will return at dawn and if they find you here they will kill you. We can only rest here for an hour in the evening and become little boys again for a while."

"How can I help you?" asked the girl.

"It's too difficult," they told her. "You would have to spend six years without speaking and you would have to make six shirts for us out of the flowers of the field. But if you said just one word, you would have to start all over again."

By the time the boys had turned back into swans and flown off, the little girl had made up her mind to save them. Then she ran into the woods and slept on the bough of a tree.

Next morning she was so busy gathering flowers to make their shirts that she did not see the two hunters who were approaching her.

"Who are you?" they asked.

The girl refused to answer.

She gave them her gold chain to get rid of them but they would not go.

Then she gave them her belt of gold and her silver sandals, but the kindly hunters would not accept them and led her out of the woods.

Their master was a young king who lived nearby and they took the girl to him.

The king was astonished by her beauty even though she refused to answer any of his questions or even smile. He wanted her to live with him in the palace. For many days she wove her flowers while the king watched her with growing tenderness. And soon he married her.

The king's mother was jealous of the girl.

"I don't like a girl who never speaks."

"Why couldn't my son have married a princess instead of an unknown girl?" she asked.

A year passed and the young woman gave birth to a child. The king was very happy. But one night, the king's mother stole the child while they slept and covered the queen's mouth in blood, so that everyone would believe that she had eaten him.

"It's not true! My wife is innocent!" shouted the king. "My wife is good, she couldn't do such a horrible thing. You are accusing her because she can't speak in her own defence. But I trust her and I don't want to hear another word against her."

The following year, the young woman had a second child. But the king's mother committed the same crime: she stole the child and stained the young woman's mouth with blood.

"And what do you say now?" she said to her son the next day. "This wife of yours is a monster."

"I forbid to you to speak of her like that," shouted the king. "I'm sure there is a simple explanation for it all! My wife is innocent, of that I'm sure."

Even when the third child was born to the young queen, she continued to weave her brothers' shirts, day after day.

"What a beautiful child!" said the enraptured king looking at his little daughter. But his evil mother again stole the child and covered the young woman's mouth in blood.

This time, the king's ministers, who were most worried by the disappearance of the three royal children, said to the king:

"You are shielding your wife, but the people want justice. Put the queen on trial, and if she cannot prove her innocence, she must be punished."

The king did what he could to prove her innocence, but his wife's silence made her defence very difficult. The queen was found guilty by the court and condemned to death. How the king cried, he still loved her and believed in her innocence!

The young queen even continued weaving shirts in her cell. Her six years of silence ended on the day set for her execution and there was only one shirt sleeve left to finish. When they led her to the stake, she took the shirts with her.

They were just about to tie her to the stake, when six swans appeared in the sky and alighted next to the queen. They quickly put on the shirts and the swans once and for all turned back into her six beloved brothers. Only one brother, the one who had put on the shirt with the missing sleeve, was not fully restored.

The people who had crowded round to see the queen's execution, were amazed at such a strange sight. The king himself did not know what to think. But at last the queen was free to speak and she said:

"My dear husband, I can now tell you that I have been wrongfully accused. Your mother stole our three children and stained my mouth with blood in an attempt to prove my guilt. These young men are my six brothers and I could only save them by my silence."

The wicked mother was forced to confess where she had hidden the three children, And the very execution stake which had been prepared for the young queen was used to burn the king's mother to death.

The Clever Little Tailor

Once upon a time in a far away country there lived a most beautiful princess.

But so arrogant was she that she would marry no-one. Princes and emperors were madly in love with her and begged for her hand, but she spent her time making them look foolish.

"I'll marry you if you can solve this riddle," she would say to them. And then she would ask them questions which were impossible to answer. Her suitors failed the test and she was able to laugh at them.

She felt so confident that no-one would ever be able to solve her riddles that one day she ordered the following proclamation to be published:

"Her Royal Highness, the Princess, will take for a husband any man who can correctly answer the riddle she sets him. The candidate's age, appearance, wealth or lack of wealth matters not."

Close to the palace in a poor but clean, little cottage lived three tailor brothers. While they sewed they idly talked of trying their luck.

"I think I could come up with the right answer," said the eldest brother. "I never miss a stitch when I'm sewing."

"I'm the same," said the middle brother. "I think I would be able to answer the princess's riddle."

The youngest brother said nothing and as he was a rather modest boy he just kept on sewing.

The two brothers talked so excitedly about the challenge that one day they decided to try their luck.

"Wait for us here. We won't be long and then one of us will return as a prince," they said to their little brother.

"I'm coming too," said the youngster.

The two brothers laughed at him but as they could not persuade him to stay behind they all went off together.

"You are a stubborn one! You are going to make a fool of yourself. But before you do, listen to us: don't start complaining afterwards if you don't have any luck," shouted the two brothers.

The princess was told that three new suitors wished to be put to the test.

"More idiots!" laughed the maiden. "I will make fools of them, just as I have with the rest. Let them go into the garden, I will receive them there, in the presence of my father's ministers."

The three brothers stood before the princess who asked the first:
"I have two kinds of hair on my head. What colours are they?"

"This isn't a very difficult riddle for me," said the elder brother. "If your hair is two colours, some must be black and the rest white."

"You haven't solved it!" exclaimed the princess. "Let's see if your brother is any sharper!"

"I know the answer. Some of your hair is brown and the rest is blonde," said the second tailor.

"You haven't guessed it either!" laughed the maiden clapping her hands with glee. "You, little tailor with the bright face, what do you say?"

The youngest tailor looked pityingly at his brothers and said to the princess:

"Neither, black nor white, nor brown, nor blonde. Your hair is the colour of gold and silver."

The princess was dumbfounded. He was exactly right. The king's ministers were watching the princess's face and guessed what had happened.

"At last someone has solved the riddle," said the most senior minister. "This time it is marriage."

Meanwhile, the princess had managed to recover from the shock.

"It's true, little tailor. You have solved the riddle; but if you want to be my husband there is another task for you.

Tonight you must sleep in the stable where my father keeps a wild bear. If you are still alive tomorrow, then I will marry you straight away."

The little tailor pretended not to be afraid and very calmly said: "Whatever you wish! But when people annoy me I become very angry indeed. So if you value the life of your father's bear, you had better behave nicely to me. It is getting rather late, please take me to the stable."

The princess was amazed by the plucky tailor and ordered one of her servants to conduct him to the stable and then went to her chambers.

For his part, the little tailor soon found himself all alone with the wild beast. Pretending to be calm, he said to the bear:

"Good evening. I am going to sleep here tonight, so we had better get to know each other."

Before the bear had time to move, he took a nut out of his pocket, cracked it open and began to eat it with great gusto. The hungry animal for-

got to be ferocious and said:

"Will you give me a nut?"

"Yes, of course!" answered the boy. "As you are sharing your stable with me, I will give you something to eat."

187

The little tailor reached into his pocket and gave the bear a handful. However, they were not nuts, but little stones which he carried for his own protection.

The bear put a stone into its mouth to crack it open as it had seen the boy do, but all it did was break one of its teeth.

"I can't open them!" growled the bear.

"I will do it for you," said the tailor, giving it one of his own which was a real nut. "But you will have to crack open the rest yourself!" he warned.

The bear greedily ate the nut that the tailor had opened and then tried harder than ever to crack open the stones it thought were nuts.

After a while, the bear did not have a tooth left in its head.

Then, the little tailor took a violin out of his sack and began to play a happy tune. The bear was delighted by the music and, forgetting the nuts, said to the boy:

"Is it hard to play the violin?"

"Of course not!"

"Can you give me a lesson?" begged the bear. "I like dancing and if I knew how to play an instrument, you could dance with me."

"I would be delighted!" said the tailor. "But first you must cut your claws, otherwise you won't be able to pluck the strings properly."

The bear believed the tailor and the boy cut its claws with a pair of scissors from his sack.

When the bear had finished the boy walked over to one corner of the stable, made himself a bed of straw and settled down to sleep upon it.

"But, what are you doing?" said the startled bear.

"Can't you see? I am trying to sleep. Leave me alone and don't bother me again with your stupidity!" said the boy closing his eyes.

In a blind rage the bear lumbered towards the youth, but then it remembered it had neither teeth nor claws and growled in anguish all night long.

Very early next morning as the princess ran to the stable she heard the bear growling and thought:

"What a shame, the bear must surely have eaten him!"

But when she saw the boy safe and well she finally realised that he was worthy of being her husband.

The tailor knew full well that his bride was still too arrogant and that she could cause problems, so he said to her:

"Do you see how I was able to control the bear?

Well, it would be easier still for me to control a wife if she ever became too arrogant."

The princess was very well behaved. At first this was because she feared him but later because she loved him and the couple lived happily ever after.

THE END